Refugees on the Run

BOOK 27

CHRIS BRACK AND SHEILA SEIFERT
ILLUSTRATIONS BY SERGIO CARIELLO

A Focus on the Family Resource
Published by Tyndale House Publishers

This book is dedicated to:

Karen, Lois, and David—
You have a special place in our hearts.

Refugees on the Run

A Focus on the Family book published by Tyndale House Publishers, Carol Stream, Illinois 60188

Cover design by Michael Heath | Magnus Creative

For Library of Congress Cataloging-in-Publication Data for this title, visit http://www.loc.gov/help/contact-general.html.

For manufacturing information regarding this product, please call 1-855-277-9400.

For information about special discounts for bulk purchases, please contact Tyndale House Publishers at csresponse@tyndale.com, or call 1-855-277- 9400.

Printed in the United States of America

ISBN: 978-1-58997-995-6

27 26 25 24 23 22 21
7 6 5 4 3 2 1

Contents

Prologue

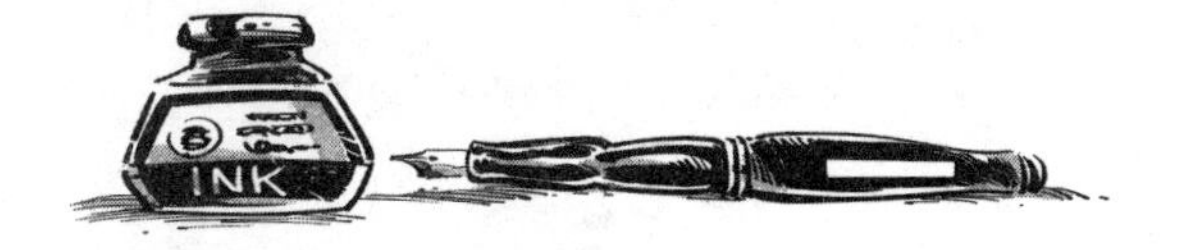

In their last two adventures—*Poison at the Pump* and *Swept into the Sea*—Patrick and Beth have had trouble with the Imagination Station.

The Model T car has a bubbling mixture of liquids in a container in its engine. But the glass container is cracked. The bubbling mixture is leaking.

The cousins must find three liquids to refill

it. They found the first liquid in London during a cholera epidemic. Then they were shipwrecked with the apostle Paul. That's where they found the second liquid. They still need to find the last liquid.

Mr. Whittaker gave Patrick a small black box with a wand. On the top of the box was a light that looked like a button. The cousins test liquids by dipping the wand into them. The right liquid will turn the light green.

Here's how their last adventure ended.

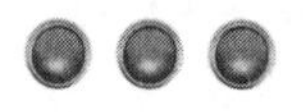

Patrick heard the hum of the Imagination Station.

"There it is," Beth said.

It appeared in front of them.

Beth jumped into the driver's seat.

Patrick hopped into the passenger side.

A small key was in the lock next to an open compartment. Patrick put the vial with the seed oil into it. He turned the key in the lock.

A sliding panel covered the compartment. Then the panel opened. The container full of oil was no longer there. The oil was now inside the Imagination Station.

Patrick left the key in the lock. They had found two of the liquids the Imagination Station needed. Patrick couldn't wait to tell Whit about this adventure.

"Let's see if we can make it home this time," Beth said. She hit the red button in the middle of the steering wheel. Nothing happened.

Then slowly the sunlight dimmed around them.

Had the Imagination Station finally broken? Patrick wondered. It felt like they were stuck in an empty tunnel.

Suddenly, the Imagination Station took off at top speed. Lights flashed all around them. A long and slow whistle blew.

The flashing lights began to swirl. Patrick saw an image of Mr. Whittaker tinkering in his workshop.

"We're almost home!" Patrick cried.

The image grew blurry. Colorful dots swirled around them.

"No!" Beth yelled.

Patrick smelled apricots, lemons, oranges, and Bambinella pears.

Then everything went black.

Destination Unknown

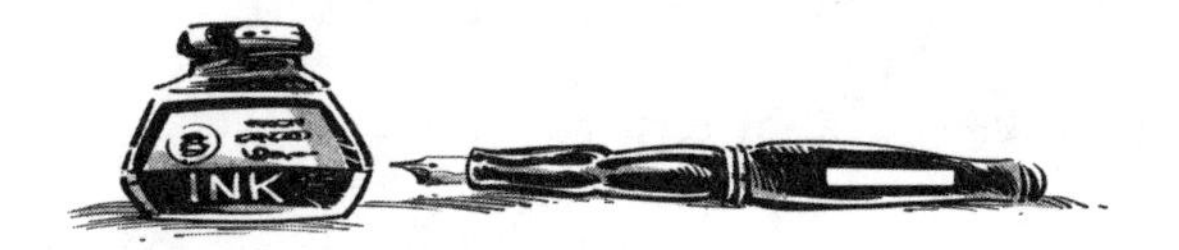

Patrick opened his eyes. The Imagination Station had landed next to a one-car garage. He looked around. Green grass was on both sides of the gravel driveway.

"Cool car," Patrick said. A shiny black automobile was parked in front of the garage. Patrick knew it was an olden-time car. He didn't know how old though.

Patrick looked for clues. "Can you read the sign on the car's front bumper?" he asked.

Beth sat in the driver's seat of the Imagination Station. She leaned forward. "It says, 'Service Consulate Japan,'" she said. "What does *consulate* mean?"

Patrick knew the word *service* meant to help someone. He knew Japan was a country. But what was a consulate?

"I don't know," he said. "Maybe it's a type of Japanese car."

"Maybe," Beth said. But she didn't look convinced.

"The third liquid for the Imagination Station must be here," Patrick said.

"We've been gone a long time. I hope we find it soon," Beth said. "We need it to fix the Imagination Station."

Patrick agreed. He unhooked his seat belt and hopped out of the Model T.

Beth did too.

Patrick looked at the white garage. It had

two wood doors. The doors reminded Patrick of gates that met in the middle.

"What a pretty green dress," Beth said. She twirled. Her skirt fanned out around her. Then it fell back to her knees. Two braids tied with green bows fell over her shoulders.

"You look like you're going to a party," Patrick said.

Beth laughed. "It's such a beautiful day," she said. "Maybe it's an outdoor birthday party. You look like you're going too."

Patrick looked down. He wore a gray vest over a green-gray shirt. He had on dark shorts. Brown knee socks covered his calves. The end of a black tie was tucked into his vest.

Patrick removed the cap on his head to look at it. It was made of gray cloth. The top of it was squashed flat against the visor. He put his hat back on his head.

The Imagination Station flickered. Then it disappeared.

"Wow! Look at that enormous house," Beth said. She pointed.

Patrick turned. Behind them was a large, white house. The bottom story looked halfway underground. The top story seemed to have a slanted roof as its ceiling. There was another level between the top and bottom.

Patrick didn't see anything exciting about it. It was just a building.

"Did the Imagination Station give you any gifts?" Patrick asked.

"Let me see," Beth said. She checked her pockets and pulled out a half sheet of paper. She showed it to her cousin.

Patrick read aloud, "Lith-oo-way-nee-a Passport, 1940." The names *B. and P. Schmidt* were below that. There was an ink stamp on it. Other words were written underneath. They were difficult to read.

"The only words I can make out are 'Dutch colony,'" Beth said.

"I wonder who the Schmidts are," Patrick said.

"We might be the Schmidts," Beth said. She sounded excited. "These are our initials. B is for Beth, and P is for Patrick."

"Hello, Beth Schmidt," Patrick said.

The cousins laughed.

"Maybe the Imagination Station gave me something too," Patrick said. He slid his hands into his pockets and took out Whit's gadget. "We'll need this to find the third liquid." He also pulled out an ink bottle.

"The Imagination Station gives us gifts we'll need," Beth said. "So we must need a passport and ink."

"People use passports to go to other countries," Patrick said. He opened the ink bottle. He dipped the wand of the gadget into it. The light didn't turn green.

"That isn't the liquid the Imagination Station needs," Beth said.

Patrick closed the ink bottle. Then he wiped the wand of the gadget on the grass.

"Maybe we need this passport to go to another country," Beth said.

Patrick nodded. "You also need a passport to get back into your country," he said. He returned the gadget and the ink bottle to his pockets.

Suddenly, a piercing scream filled the air. Then a woman's voice yelled, "I'm being crushed!"

Beth took off running.

Patrick followed.

They ran around the large, white building toward the scream.

The Gate

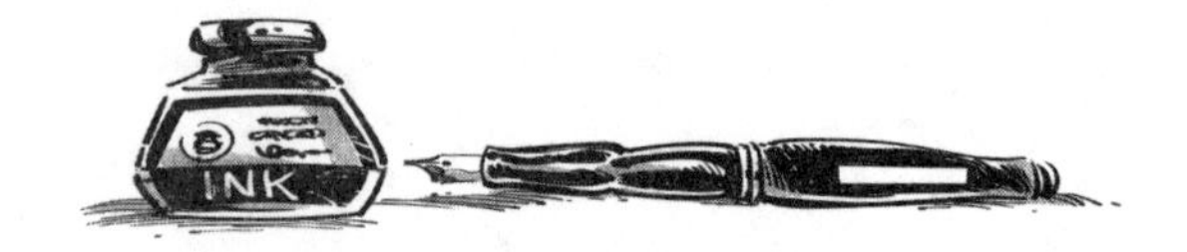

Beth turned the corner to the front of the house. She stopped.

Patrick bumped into her. “What’s up?” he asked.

Beth pointed. An iron fence circled the white building. A crowd of people stood outside the fence. The crowd was pushing the gate open.

Only one man was inside the fence with Beth and Patrick. The man wore a gray suit and hat. He was pushing on the gate to keep it from opening more.

"Hurry," the man said. "Step through, Agnes."

Beth thought, *That man wants only the one lady to enter.*

Agnes wore a brown dress and white apron. She had a large straw basket in her hands. It was too big to fit through the opening.

The crowd outside the fence pushed her forward.

Agnes screamed again.

Patrick hurried toward the man. "Can we help?" he asked.

Agnes yelled, "Boris!"

Faces peeked between the black metal bars of the fence.

"Hold the gate with me," Boris said.

Patrick grasped two of the metal bars.

"Take my basket," Agnes said.

Beth hurried to the opening.

This crowd wasn't like any Beth had ever seen. The men wore hats, suits, and ties. The women were in dresses that went just below their knees. They wore hats or scarves over their hair. Most had suitcases in their hands or by their feet.

"The basket is too big," Beth said. "Toss it over the fence." She took a step back to catch it.

Agnes lifted the empty basket above her. She tossed it over the fence.

Beth caught the basket and set it on the ground. She hurried back to the woman.

Agnes shoved one foot through the gate. The rest of her body was still outside.

"Once she gets through," Boris said, "slam the gate shut."

"Okay," Patrick said.

"You," Boris said to Beth. "Take the cook's hands. Pull her back onto consulate grounds."

Beth nodded. She realized this fenced-in

building must be called a consulate. But she still didn't know what that meant.

"Ready?" Beth asked. She grabbed the woman's hands. "One, two, three." Beth pulled with all her might. The cook popped through the opening.

Beth almost lost her balance. She released the woman's hands. Then she grabbed at the gate to steady herself.

Two people in the crowd grabbed Beth's hand.

"Pull us through," one said.

Patrick and Boris strained to shut the gate.

The hands pulled Beth forward.

She struggled. But the hands didn't let go.

Suddenly Beth popped through the gap and was outside the gate.

The gate snapped shut behind her.

Beth fell to the ground. "Ow," she said.

"Open the gate!" Patrick yelled. "My cousin is on the other side!"

"Don't open it!" Agnes yelled.

"We can't open it," Boris said. "The only way to help your cousin is to talk to the consul."

"Then take me to the consul!" Patrick said.

"Very well," Boris said. "I'm not sure how you got inside the fence. But you helped me. Now I'll help you."

"Don't worry, Beth," Patrick yelled. "I'll convince the consul to open the gate."

"Okay," Beth said. She tried to stand. But the crowd was too tight.

Boris yelled, "Find a safe place, young lady. This might take some time to sort out." He and Agnes turned from the gate and walked toward the building.

Patrick looked at Beth.

Beth waved at him to follow Boris.

The crowd still pressed against her. They didn't look mean. They looked worried and disappointed.

Beth watched Boris, Agnes, and Patrick go into the big house. The door shut behind them. But no one in the crowd walked away. They stayed behind the fence.

Beth heard someone in the crowd ask, "What should we do now?"

"Take my hands," a girl close to Beth's age said. Her dark-brown eyes sparkled. A light breeze moved her dark curls. The girl's dress matched the color of the sky.

Beth was glad to see a friendly face in the crowd. She grabbed the girl's hands.

The girl easily pulled Beth to her feet.

"Thank you," Beth said. "My name is Beth."

"My name is Leza," the girl said.

Beth looked around. The consulate was on one side of the cobblestone street. There was a park on the other side of the street.

"How did you get on consulate grounds?" Leza asked.

"I was there with my cousin," Beth said.

"But how did you get on that side of the fence?" she asked. "The Japanese consulate hasn't let anyone in."

A man and woman behind Leza turned their heads. They looked at Beth. She wondered if they were listening.

"I don't know exactly," Beth said. "But my cousin will try to get the consul to let me in."

"That's great news," Leza said. She beamed.

"Who is your friend?" the woman behind Leza asked. Her dress looked like Leza's, only faded. She wore a tan scarf wrapped around her dark hair.

"This is Beth," Leza said. "Her cousin is in the consulate right now. Beth, this is my mother, and that is my father."

"Nice to meet you," Beth said.

"It's a pleasure to meet you also," Leza's father said. "Where are your parents?"

"They aren't here," Beth said. "My cousin and I are on our own."

Leza's parents gave each other worried looks.

Beth turned toward the crowd. "Why are so many people waiting here?" she asked.

"We all want to leave Lithuania," Leza said.

Beth recognized that word. *Lithuania* was written on her passport from the Imagination Station.

Lithuania must be a country, Beth thought. "Is Lithuania a bad place to live?" she asked.

"Oh no," Leza said. "It's a wonderful place." She leaned closer to Beth's ear. "But the Nazis are coming. They want to hurt all Jews. My family and I are Jewish."

The Crowd

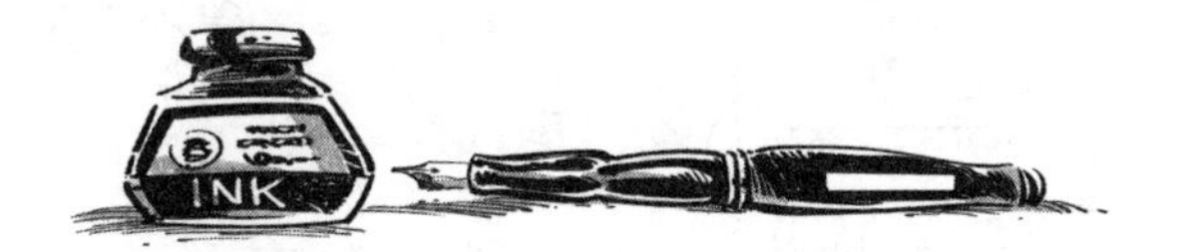

Patrick entered the consulate behind Boris. He hadn't figured out what a consulate was. But he had figured out that the consul was a person.

"This way," Boris said. He led Patrick down a hall.

"What do you do here?" Patrick asked.

"I help the consul," Boris said.

"You're the consul's assistant?" Patrick asked.

Boris nodded.

Patrick followed Boris into a living room.

A Japanese man sat on a dark-brown couch. He wore a suit and a tie.

Boris removed his hat. "Good morning," Boris said with a low bow.

Patrick took off his hat too. He bowed.

"Good morning," the Japanese man said. He leaned forward in a small bow. A vase of flowers sat on a coffee table in front of him.

"May I present Patrick?" Boris said. "He helped the cook get back on consulate grounds."

The Japanese man said, "Thank you for helping."

"You're welcome," Patrick said. "I would like to speak with the consul or the consulate."

The man said, "You won't be able to talk to the consulate."

Boris laughed. "This building is a consulate," he said. "Inside the gate belongs to Japan. Outside the gate belongs to Lithuania."

"Oh," Patrick said. "A consulate is an office that one country has inside another country."

The older man smiled and nodded his head. "I am the consul. I represent Japan here," he said. "My name is Chiune Sugihara."

"It's nice to meet you, Shy-yoon Su-ji-har-a," Patrick said.

The consul laughed. "You can call me Sempo," he said. "It's my nickname and easier to say."

"Thank you, Sempo," Patrick said.

Sempo nodded toward the window. "What did you find out?" he asked Boris.

"They're Jews," Boris said. "Most have escaped from Poland."

"They weren't here last night," Sempo said. He sighed. "The Nazis must have taken control of

Poland. These people are now refugees. They no longer have a country of their own."

"But why are they here?" Patrick asked. "My cousin is in that crowd."

"They want to leave Lithuania," Sempo said. "Is your cousin Jewish?"

"No," Patrick said. "She is a Christian. But she was pulled through the gate."

Sempo's forehead wrinkled. "That is unfortunate," he said.

"Can we open the gate for her?" Patrick asked.

Sempo shook his head. "The gate must remain shut for now," he said. "But somehow I will try to help her and the others."

A Japanese woman wearing a colorful silk robe entered the room. Her black hair was pulled back from her face.

"Patrick, this is my wife, Yukiko," Sempo said.

Patrick bowed low. "Good morning," he said.

Boris bowed too.

"Good morning," she said and bowed.

A yellow cat with a striped tail rushed into the room.

A laughing boy chased after it. He wore a short-sleeved, white, button-up shirt. He also wore shorts and knee socks.

"That is my five-year-old son, Hiroki," Sempo said. "He finds Mei, our cat, intriguing. She does not favor him."

The cat jumped onto the couch. Hiroki jumped up too.

"Get down," Yukiko said in a firm voice. "The couch is not for wild boys." The cat jumped down and moved toward Patrick.

"I'm sorry, Mother," Hiroki said. He slowly climbed down and bowed his head low. Then he walked over to Sempo.

"Why are all those people outside, Father?" Hiroki asked.

"They want to leave Lithuania," Sempo said. "Bad people are chasing them. The bad people want to hurt them."

"Will you help them?" Hiroki asked.

Sempo ruffled his son's hair. "I can only do what Japan says I can," he said. "I represent a whole country."

Mei began to purr. Patrick reached down to pet her.

A young woman hurried into the room. She was dressed much like Yukiko, but her robe was a different color. A baby was in her arms and another little boy followed her.

Hiroki walked over to Patrick. He whispered, "That is Aunt Setsuko and my younger brothers. She is our nanny."

The boy reached out his hands to grab the cat.

Mei jumped onto the coffee table.

Hiroki frowned.

Aunt Setsuko bounced the baby. “What does the crowd want?” she asked.

“They want visas to leave Lithuania,” Sempo said.

Patrick whispered, “What is a visa?”

Hiroki shrugged.

“A visa gives permission to travel through a country,” Sempo said. He smiled at Patrick.

“My cousin and I have a passport,” Patrick said. “Isn’t that enough?”

“No,” Sempo said. “You also need a place to go. A passport is from your country. A visa is for traveling through another country.”

“The Dutch consulate gave many Jewish people a destination stamp,” Boris said. “They are going to a Dutch colony.”

“So, then all they need are visas,” he said.

Boris, Yukiko, Aunt Setsuko, and Sempo nodded.

The baby cooed.

"Who are the bad people chasing them?" Hiroki asked.

"The Nazis," Boris said. "They do not want there to be any Jewish people."

Aunt Setsuko gasped. "Surely they wouldn't hurt children," she said.

"They would," Boris said.

Sempo put his hand on his chin. "I'll ask for permission to give out visas," he said.

"That will take a long time," Hiroki said. "Japan is far from here. There is Russia, and then water, and then Japan."

Sempo smiled at his son. "I will use a teleprinter. It is like a telegraph machine," Sempo said. "It's a quick way to send messages."

Sempo and Boris moved toward the door.

Patrick looked out the window. He didn't see Beth. But he did see children in the crowd.

Patrick hurried after Sempo. Patrick hoped the teleprinter worked fast. He didn't want anything bad to happen to those kids.

Rocks and Refugees

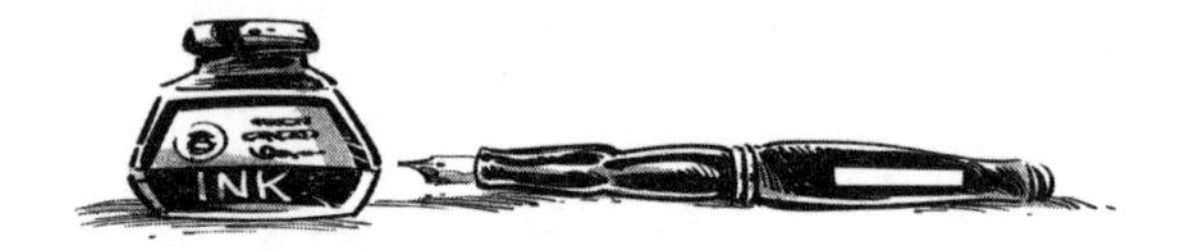

Beth looked at Leza's father. He looked like the other men in the crowd. He wore a brown suit and hat. But Leza's parents didn't carry suitcases like the others.

"We are Jews," her father said simply. "Nazis don't like Jews."

Beth shuddered. She'd met Nazis in an earlier adventure. She remembered that

Hitler's mean soldiers had searched for Jewish people.

Leza's father said, "The gates won't open again today. We should go to the Russian consulate. Maybe they can help us."

"It was nice meeting you," Beth said.

"Beth, you may come with us," Leza's mother said. "You shouldn't stay here without parents."

Leza grabbed Beth's hand. "Come with us to the Russian consulate," she said. "Then we'll go to my house. It isn't too far."

Beth remembered what Boris said. He had told her to find a safe place.

"Is this crowd dangerous?" Beth asked.

"The crowd isn't dangerous," Leza's father said. "But others are."

Leza's home seemed like a safe place. "Thank you," Beth said. "I'd be happy to go with you."

Leza's mother and father began crossing the cobblestone street toward the park.

Beth and Leza followed.

"Do you know the people in that crowd?" Beth asked.

Leza shook her head. "No. Most of them have come from another country called Poland," she said. "My Uncle Hadja came from Poland. He and his family had to sneak out of Poland at night."

They entered the park. It was filled with trees.

"How can the consul help everyone?" Beth asked.

Leza's mother looked back at them. "The Japanese consul can issue visas," she said. "Now keep up."

Leza and Beth hurried forward.

Beth was still a little confused. "I thought all you needed was a passport," Beth said. "What's a visa?"

Leza laughed. “You must have a visa stamp in your passport. Then you can travel through other countries,” she said.

Beth said, “So, a visa stamp gives you permission to travel.”

“That’s right,” Leza’s mother said.

Ping!

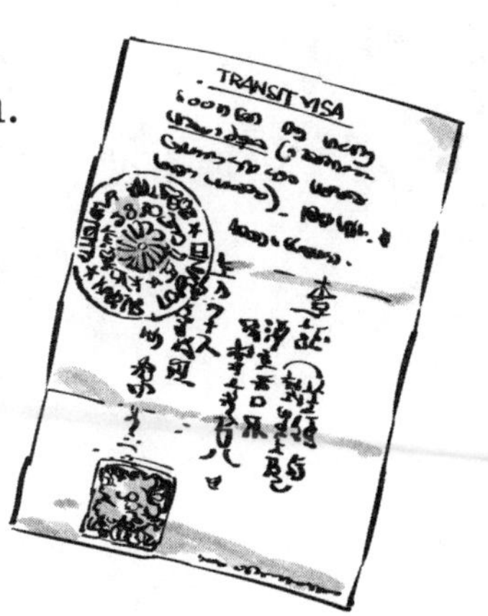

A rock hit a tree near them.

A faraway dog barked.

“Where will you go when you leave Lithuania?” Beth asked.

“We can’t go west,” Leza said. “The Baltic Sea is to the west. The Nazis watch it carefully.”

A red squirrel scurried up a pine tree.

“Which direction is Poland?” Beth asked.

Ping!

Another rock bounced off a nearby tree. A schoolboy ran to hide behind an oak tree.

That rock almost hit us, Beth thought.

"Poland is to the south," Leza said. "We can't go that way either. The Nazis are already there."

The west and south were closed to Leza's family. "You would have to go north or east," Beth said.

Another boy ran from behind a birch tree and threw a rock. "Go back to Poland!" he yelled. He dove behind a large bush.

The rock fell short.

Other boys laughed.

"Papa?" Leza said quietly.

"I am here," Leza's dad said. "Ignore them."

Beth couldn't believe her ears. "But they're throwing rocks at us!" she said.

Leza's dad said, "Some people don't like Jews. Don't pay any attention to them."

Beth wanted to shake her fist at the

schoolboys. But she didn't. Instead, she asked, "Are those boys Nazis?"

"No. But the Nazis lie on the radio," Leza's mother said. "They say things like 'Jews take your jobs and money.' It isn't true. But our neighbors are beginning to believe them."

"That's terrible," Beth said. They walked in silence for a while. Another rock hit the ground near Beth's feet.

Beth was glad the boys were bad shots. "Will you go north?" she asked.

Leza's father sighed. "No," he said. "The Nazis will go north to the small country of Latvia next."

They left the park and were in a neighborhood with many houses.

"We must go east," Leza said, "to Japan. Then we'll travel by boat to a Dutch colony near South America."

Beth remembered that "Dutch colony" was

on her and Patrick's passport. "Japan is to the east," she said. "But aren't there other countries between here and there?"

Leza's mother nodded. She said, "We need to travel through Russia to get to Japan. But we need permission to travel through Russia. The Japanese consul must ask the Russians for permission."

The trip sounded complicated to Beth.

"My parents got a passport when they were first married," Leza said. "My grandparents and I don't have passports."

They all walked past a butcher shop.

"Can you get a passport?" Beth asked.

"We don't know," Leza said.

Next to the butcher shop was a fresh-fruit stand.

"The Russians are now in charge of Lithuania," Leza's father said. "They want all Lithuanians to stay in Lithuania. If we pay a lot of money, they might let us leave."

"Do you have a lot of money?" Beth asked.

"We will once Father sells his clock shop," Leza said.

"Don't the Russians know you're in danger?" Beth asked.

Leza's father huffed.

"They don't care," Leza said.

Beth shook her head. A bakery's delicious smells filled the air. But it didn't make her feel better. Leza and her family were in trouble. And it seemed like no one wanted to help them.

Permission

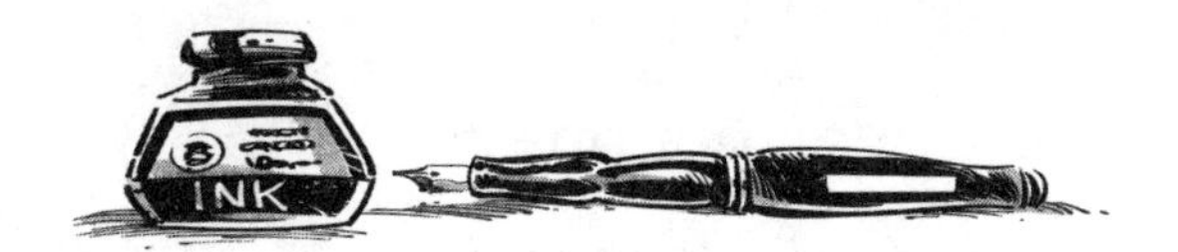

Patrick followed Boris into Sempo's office.

The consul sat in a chair facing a machine that looked like an old typewriter. But it had more cylinders, shiny metal compartments, and moving parts.

Patrick studied the teleprinter as Sempo finished typing.

"Does Sempo know Morse code?" Patrick asked.

Boris shook his head. "He has a teleprinter. It can send and receive text."

Sempo tapped out his message. Then he turned his chair toward them. "It's done," he said. "I should know Japan's decision soon."

Geography was not one of Patrick's favorite subjects. But he did know that Japan was a group of islands far away.

Patrick asked, "How can refugees in Lithuania travel to Japan?"

Boris said, "They will have to take a train through Russia first."

Patrick sighed. Giving out visas was complicated. He hoped Beth was safe. It might take a while for the consulate to open its gate.

"First, Japan must give me permission

to give out visas," Sempo said. "I'll go to the Russian consulate while I'm waiting. I need to know if Russia will honor the visas I give."

"I hope they both say yes," Patrick said.

Sempo stood. "As do I," he said. "Would you like to go with Boris and me?"

Boris opened the door for Sempo.

"Yes," Patrick said. He wanted to stay close to Sempo. If Japan gave Sempo permission to give visas, the gates could open. Patrick wanted to be ready when that happened.

Patrick, Boris, and Sempo didn't go out the front door. Instead, they went out the back door and walked toward the garage. There was no crowd at the back of the house.

Sempo opened the back door of his black car. He gestured for Patrick to get in.

I get to ride in the cool car! Patrick thought. Patrick hopped into the back seat. He pulled the door shut.

Sempo slid into the driver's seat and started the car. Boris opened a gate and slipped into the passenger seat.

The car took off with a roar.

Patrick bounced up and down on the springy seat.

Soon Sempo turned onto a wide street with large buildings. Patrick looked back to see the crowd at the Japanese consulate. But they were too far away.

Finally, Sempo parked in front of an official-looking building. There was a long line of people waiting to get in.

Soldiers in olive-colored uniforms with black belts stood at attention. Their pants were tucked into black boots.

Sempo got out of the car. He led the way through the line of people. Patrick and Boris followed him inside the building.

"Sempo," a man called out with a wave.

The man wore a white shirt and a dark tie. His hair was greased back. Dark circles were under his eyes.

"Jan," Sempo said. He bowed.

Jan bowed in return. "I'm glad to see you one last time," he said.

Boris whispered to Patrick, "This man is the Dutch consul."

"Where are you going?" Sempo asked Jan.

"The Russians closed my consulate," Jan said. "I'm leaving Lithuania. They'll close yours soon."

Patrick couldn't believe it. The Russians

were closing consulates in Lithuania. How would the Jews get the visas they needed? How would he find Beth if the Japanese consulate closed?

"That is bad news," Sempo said. "Crowds of people are outside my consulate. They are asking for visas. I have to know if Russia will honor Japan's visas."

"You are a good man, Sempo," Jan said. "I wish you well." He bowed low.

Sempo returned the bow. "Perhaps we will work together again someday," Sempo said.

Jan gave him a nod and a smile. Then he turned and left.

Sempo led Boris and Patrick to the back of the lobby. They stopped at a door. Hallways led away from that door.

"Wait out here," Sempo said. "Russian officials like to speak to only one person at a time. Keep watch. I'd like to know what else is going on."

"We'll split up and listen," Boris said. He pointed down a hallway. "Patrick, you go that way." He pointed down another. "I'll go this way."

"Good," Sempo said. He went through the door.

Patrick walked down a dimly lit hallway.

People were everywhere. Some looked scared. Others looked upset. No one looked happy.

Dark wood panels were on either side of him. They made the hallway feel formal and cold.

An older man with a wrinkly face walked out of a door. "That's that," he muttered. He walked past Patrick.

What was what? Patrick wondered. He said, "Excuse me."

The man turned around.

"What's wrong?" Patrick asked.

The man said, "The Russians say I'm too old to get a passport." He turned away. "We never should have let the Russians run Lithuania."

A couple with a dark-haired girl walked out of the same office. Next to them was a girl in a green dress.

"Beth!" Patrick said.

"Patrick!" Beth said. "Leza, this is my cousin. Patrick, this is Leza and her parents."

"Hello," Patrick said. He turned to Beth. "What are you doing here?"

"We tried to get a passport for Leza and her grandparents," Beth said.

"They denied our request," Leza's father said.

Patrick thought about the older man. "Let me guess," Patrick said. "Leza is too young. Her grandparents are too old."

Leza's mother said, "That is exactly what they said. They won't issue new passports. They will not add their names to our passport. There isn't enough room on it."

Her words gave Patrick an idea. "Beth, I need our passport. Leza, take your father's money," Patrick said, "and come with me." He hoped his plan would work.

6

Passport Problems

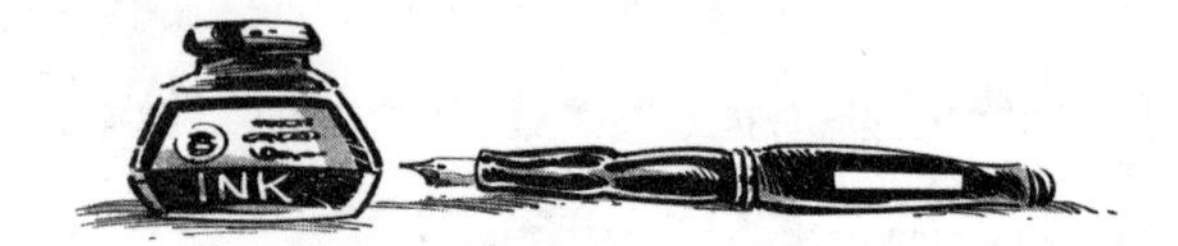

Patrick and Leza stood in front of a Russian official. Patrick held his and Beth's passport. Leza held her father's money.

Sempo had said that Russians liked to speak with one person at a time. Maybe this man would allow two.

The Russian official said, "The girl and her grandparents can't be added to the parents' passport. Next."

"Her parents will leave the country," Patrick said. "But her grandparents are old. They might not be able to take care of her. Is Russia prepared to take care of orphans?"

The man gave Patrick a long look. "Do you think it would help Russia if we gave her a passport?" he asked. He waved his hand in the air. "There is no room on her parents' passport."

"There's room on this one," Patrick said. He slid his and Beth's passport onto the desk.

The man read it. "What is your name, girl?" he asked.

"Leza Schmidt," she said.

Patrick almost laughed out loud. Her last name was the same as the one on their passport. The Imagination Station had given Beth the perfect gift.

Leza put her father's money on the desk.

The official slid the money into his own pocket. He wrote on the passport, stamped it, and signed it.

"Thank you," Leza said.

Patrick picked up the passport and hurried out of the room.

Leza followed him.

The door shut behind them.

Patrick held up the passport. "Leza has been added to our passport," he said. He handed it back to Beth.

Her mother clapped. "That's wonderful!" she said.

Leza's father smiled happily.

Beth put the passport in her pocket and laughed. "I'm so glad!" she said.

"How will we pay for a passport for my grandparents?" Leza said.

"Don't worry," Leza's father said. He put his hand on her shoulder.

"We'll have plenty of money," Leza's mother said, "once the shop sells."

A Russian soldier walked toward them. "No standing in the hall," he said. He herded their group and others back to the main lobby.

Patrick saw Boris. He waved.

Boris hurried to him.

Patrick said, "Did you hear anything?"

"No," Boris said. "Did you?"

Patrick shook his head no.

Russian soldiers pushed them toward the front door.

Soon they were all on the sidewalk.

"Boris," Patrick said. "This is my cousin Beth, her friend Leza, and Leza's parents."

"Hello," Boris said.

"Very nice to meet you," Leza's mother and father said together.

"They are trying to leave Lithuania," Patrick said.

Leza's father said, "We have passports. But we need visas."

"The Japanese consul is working on that," Boris said.

Boris turned to Patrick. "I will go with Sempo," he said. "You have found your cousin. You should stay with her."

"No," Leza's father said. He pointed to Patrick. "You must help Sempo. He will need help to give visas to so many."

"Patrick, would you like to work for me for a few days?" Boris asked.

Patrick looked at Beth. They would be separated again. And they still needed to find a liquid for the Imagination Station.

Beth looked at Patrick and nodded.

"I'd be happy to help," Patrick said.

Beth was glad. It was important to help as

many people as they could. Then they'd find the third liquid.

Sempo was at his car.

Beth watched Patrick and Boris walk to the car.

"Leza," her mother said. "Go tell your grandparents your good news."

"Tell them we'll try to find their visas through other consulates," her father said.

Leza nodded. She led Beth down one block and up another.

The girls passed the bakery and the fresh-fruit stand. Then they passed the butcher shop, a seamstress shop, and an alley. They turned a corner and walked down another block. Pearl's Tea Shop was in front of them.

Leza opened the door. A bell over the door jingled. The girls entered the small shop.

A small, wrinkly faced woman was at the counter. Her gray hair was pulled back in a bun. A red shawl covered her shoulders. She handed a package of tea to a girl around their age.

"It was nice to meet you, Gabby," the woman said. "Welcome to Lithuania. I hope you enjoy the tea."

Beth and Leza walked between the wood tables. All the chairs were empty. There were no customers drinking pots of hot tea today.

"Thank you," Gabby said. She didn't look at Beth and Leza. Instead, she kept her head down and hurried out the door.

The older woman saw them. "Leza!" she said.

Leza hurried to her grandmother and gave her a hug.

Teacups hung on hooks behind the counter. A glass display case was filled with cakes, biscuits, and scones.

"This is my friend Beth," Leza said.

"Welcome, Beth," the woman said. "You may call me Grandma Pearl."

"Nice to meet you, Grandma Pearl," Beth said.

"Gabby was my only customer today," Grandma Pearl said. "Her family just came from Poland. Let's go in back for a chat."

The girls followed her through a door. The back room smelled of tea and old wood.

Grandma Pearl sat in a rocking chair.

"I have good news," Leza said. She sat on a chair next to her grandmother. "Beth and her cousin have a passport. My name was added to it."

Grandma Pearl smiled. She said, "Grandpa Ben is trying to get us a passport now. We'll all leave Lithuania together."

Beth sat on a nearby footstool. "That's wonderful," Beth said.

"I have more news," Grandma Pearl said.

"Your Uncle Hadja has reached the United States. He's found a position for your father as a clockmaker. Your father will need to get there soon."

Leza clapped her hands. Then she sniffed the air. "Were you making your special tea?" she asked. "When can I learn how to make it?"

Grandma Pearl laughed. "Soon," she said. "You have to be old enough to remember the ingredients."

An older man walked into the room. He was frowning.

"Grandpa Ben!" Leza said. She jumped up and gave him a hug.

His frown turned into a warm smile.

"This is my friend Beth," Leza said.

"Hello," Beth said.

"It's nice to meet you," Grandpa Ben said.

"What's wrong?" Grandma Pearl asked.

"Our friend Martin wasn't able to get us

a passport," he said. "His work at the Dutch consulate has come to an end. The consulate was closed."

Grandma Pearl sighed.

"He might know someone who will buy our tea shop," he said. "But we can't leave without passports."

"And we won't leave without you," Leza said.

This was a bigger problem than Beth had thought. No one would be able to leave Lithuania!

A Family Meeting

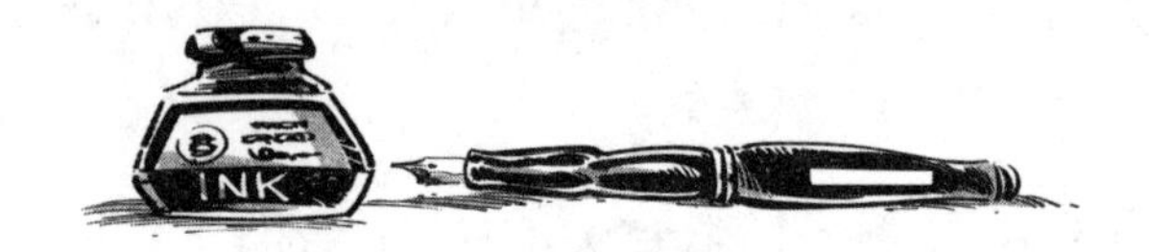

Patrick, Boris, and Sempo walked into the consulate through the back door. Patrick heard footsteps running toward them.

"Father!" Hiroki called. He waved a piece of paper. "You received a telegram!"

Yukiko was behind him. She said, "I let him take it from the teleprinter."

"You're a good helper," Sempo said. He took the slip and read it.

"Did Japan give permission?" Patrick asked.

Sempo sighed. "No," he said. "I will ask again. Yukiko, please gather the family in the living room. I'll be there shortly."

Sempo headed toward his office.

Boris and Patrick followed.

"This probably has something to do with the treaty," Boris said.

"What is a treaty?" Patrick asked. They entered Sempo's office. The consul was already using the teleprinter.

"It's an agreement," Boris said. "Japan and the Nazis want to work together."

"Why?" Patrick asked.

Sempo sent his message. "I don't know why," Sempo said with a shrug. "I do know one thing. They don't want me to put the treaty at risk."

The teleprinter started printing a message. Sempo read it aloud, "Important. Visas cannot be issued unless people have a country to go to. Travelers must have money to pay for trains and hotels."

Sempo frowned.

"That is Japan's way of saying no," Boris said to Patrick.

Sempo sent another message. His frown deepened with the next response.

Patrick shook his head. Sempo's bosses didn't want to help the refugees.

"Let's go to the living room," Sempo said. They walked to the room.

Yukiko, Setsuko, Hiroki, and one of his brothers sat on the couch. The baby was probably sleeping. They were waiting for Sempo to speak.

Sempo sat on the couch. He turned toward them.

Patrick stood by the window. The crowd outside was even larger now.

Boris stood behind the couch.

"We have a decision to make," Sempo said. "And we must all agree."

Patrick looked at Boris. Boris raised a finger to his lips.

Sempo said to Hiroki, “You have seen the people outside.”

“Yes,” Hiroki said.

“They have run away from people trying to hurt them,” he said. “They are tired, scared, and sad.”

“They can sleep in my bed,” Hiroki offered.

Sempo smiled. He said, “There are too many. But I do want to help these people.”

“Will the bad people hurt us?” Hiroki asked.

“They might,” Sempo said. “And I might get in a lot of trouble for helping the people in that crowd.” Sempo stood. He went to the window by Patrick and looked out.

Patrick held the curtains for him.

Sempo looked and then turned back to his family. “I need to know how everyone feels,” he said. “If I help, we might be in danger.”

Silence.

Then Hiroki yelled, “I will fight the bad

people with you. We will help the sad people outside."

Sempo smiled. So did Setsuko and Yukiko.

Setsuko said, "I agree with Hiroki. One day we may need help. I hope people will be brave and help us."

Yukiko said, "I want you to help them too."

Sempo nodded. "We must do what's right," he said. "If I don't help, I'd be disobeying God. But I must disobey my government to help these people."

"I want to help too," Patrick said.

Boris said, "Count me in."

"Then we are in agreement," Sempo said.

Hiroki asked, "What do you want me to do?"

"I want you to help your Aunt Setsuko pack," he said. "The Russians are shutting down consulates. We shall be asked to leave soon. Until then, I will use the garage to issue visas."

"I will help you," Yukiko said.

"No one in in my family is to help me," he said.

Patrick understood.

Sempo could get in trouble for disobeying his country. Japan, Russia, and the Nazis might be mad at him. But he didn't want anyone to be upset with his family.

The family meeting was over. Quietly, each person left, even Sempo.

"Will you help me?" Boris asked Patrick. "I need to set up an office for Sempo in the garage."

"Yes," Patrick said.

They hurried outside and walked past Sempo's shiny black car.

Boris opened one of the wooden doors to the garage.

Patrick opened the other.

Together they pushed an old desk into the middle of the room.

Patrick dusted it. The dust flew into the air.

Patrick sneezed. *Achoo!*

Boris moved a stack of papers from a shelf to the desk. He said, “Go back to the house. Bring everything on top of Sempo’s desk.”

Patrick took off running. He entered Sempo’s office. He picked up a large notebook and an official rubber stamp. Then he grabbed bottles of ink and an ink pen. He cradled them in his arms.

Patrick ran back to the garage.

The black car had been moved.

Patrick dropped everything on the desk.

“Get his chair, too,” Boris said. He started setting the supplies in place on the desk.

Patrick hurried back inside for Sempo’s chair. It was heavy. But he pushed and pulled until it was in the garage.

Boris had organized the desk. He had placed two worn crates as stools for Patrick and Boris.

Patrick asked, "Will Sempo really get in trouble for disobeying Japan?"

Boris shrugged. He said, "He might be fired as a consul."

"That's terrible," Patrick said. *How would Sempo take care of his family?* Patrick wondered.

"It could get worse," Boris said. "They might also kill him."

Sempo's Garage

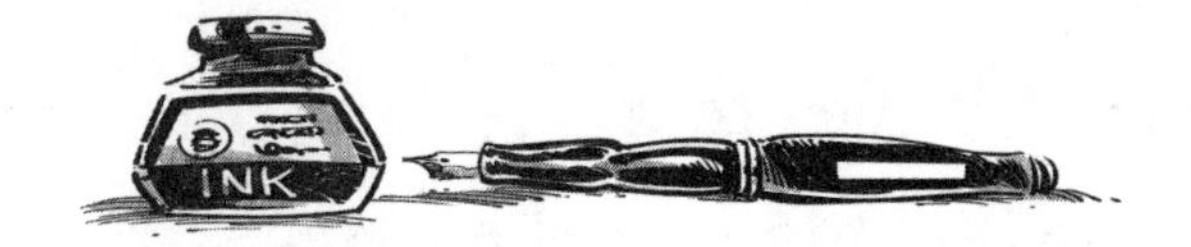

Sempo walked into the garage and sat behind the desk. "The Russian government says they'll honor Japan's visas. They'll let refugees travel through their country. But they'll also close this consulate soon."

It's a race against time, Patrick thought.

"Please open the gate," Sempo said.

Patrick and Boris jogged to the front of the house.

Boris unlocked the gate. He said loudly, "The consul will see you now."

A joyful cheer went up.

Patrick turned to walk back to the garage.

But a rush of men and women carried him forward.

Patrick felt the crowd pressing. He started to run. He had to reach the garage first.

Sempo sat behind the desk.

Refugees poured into the garage and surrounded him.

The consul raised his eyebrows.

Mei screeched. She darted between Patrick's feet.

The people in the garage were smooshed against each other.

Boris pushed his way in. "There are so many. What do we do?" he asked.

Patrick had an idea. He moved forward and waved his arms to stop the crowd.

"Quiet!" he said. "I will hand out numbers. We'll call these numbers. Only then can you speak to the consul."

Sempo smiled.

The crowd stopped shoving.

Patrick quickly wrote numbers on pieces of paper. Then he and Boris handed them to the crowd.

Sempo called, "Number one."

A family pushed their way to his desk.

"Where do you plan to go?" he asked.

"To a Dutch colony," the man and woman replied together.

"Do you have enough money for hotels, trains, and ships?" Sempo asked.

"Yes," the man said.

Patrick looked at the tired and dusty couple. They didn't look like they had any money. But they handed Sempo the fee for the visa.

Sempo wrote their names in his notebook. He wrote the necessary information on their passport. He stamped their visa with his official stamp from Japan. Then he signed it.

"Thank you," the woman whispered. "Thank you."

"Do not thank me. Thank my country," Sempo said. "Say, 'Banzai Nippon.'"

"What does that mean?" Patrick asked. He watched the first family head back through the crowd to leave.

"It means 'Long live Japan,'" Boris said. "Number two!"

The next family came forward.

Agnes walked into the garage. She carried

a tray. It held a kettle, teacups, paper-wrapped leaves, and small biscuits.

She said, "You need food and tea to keep up your strength."

"Thank you, Agnes," Boris said.

She set the tray on the shelf behind them.

Sempo nodded. "Thank you," he said. But he didn't reach for the tea or food. He kept writing.

"Number three," Boris yelled. He grabbed a biscuit and stuffed it into his mouth.

Patrick did not drink tea often. But he put a paper filled with tea leaves into his cup.

Agnes poured steaming water on the leaves.

Patrick took a sip. The liquid tasted like hot water with a hint of peppermint.

"Let the leaves soak," Agnes said. "It will taste better in a few minutes."

"Thank you," Patrick

said. He set down his cup and wrote more numbers.

Agnes pushed her way back through the crowd.

"Number four," Boris yelled as a family thanked Sempo.

Patrick looked at the tea. *Could the Imagination Station need this liquid?* he wondered. He turned away from the people. Then he took the gadget out of his pocket.

Patrick put the wand in the tea. The light flickered. But it didn't stay on.

How odd, Patrick thought. He put the gadget back in his pocket. He grabbed two tea packets and put them in his pocket too.

Maybe the tea wasn't strong enough. He would test it again later.

Patrick went back to writing numbers. Much later he asked, "How many visas have you given out?"

Sempo looked at his notebook. He said, "I have written sixteen visas." Sempo looked at his watch. "It's taken me two hours. That is too long."

"I have an idea," Patrick said. "Let's get another stamp. Then Boris and I can stamp the passports for you."

Sempo smiled. "That would help, Patrick," he said. "My hand is already tired. But you would need to take my stamp to make a new one. There's no time for that."

Boris said, "I will stamp everyone's passport."

"I'll write their names in the notebook. I can also take their money," Patrick said.

Sempo nodded. "That will save time," he said. "I'll write down their information and sign my name."

"Number seventeen," Boris yelled.

A family of six came forward.

"Where would you like to go?" Sempo asked.

"America," their little girl said.

"Do you have a destination stamp for America?" Sempo asked.

"No, we have one for a Dutch colony," the father said.

"You shall go to the Dutch colony," Sempo said. He smiled at the little girl. "From there you can go to America."

Boris stamped their passport.

Sempo filled out the information and signed it.

They paid their fee to Patrick. Then he wrote their names in the notebook.

"Number eighteen," Boris said.

Another family came forward.

Agnes returned with sandwiches at dinnertime. Patrick stuffed one in his mouth and kept working.

They worked together all evening.

Soon the sun started setting. But the line didn't shorten.

Sempo leaned forward. He dipped his pen into the inkwell. He tried to write. Nothing happened.

"The ink has run out," Sempo said.

Boris said, "All the shops are closed now. I'll buy ink in the morning."

"Then we must return tomorrow," a refugee said in a low voice.

Patrick felt awful. He shoved his hands into his pockets. He felt something. He pulled out the ink bottle from the Imagination Station.

"You don't have to," Patrick said. He handed the ink bottle to Sempo.

Sempo looked at him strangely. “I do not know how you have this. But I'm glad you do,” he said.

Eventually they would have to stop. But not yet. There were so many more visas to write.

A Lamb Shank

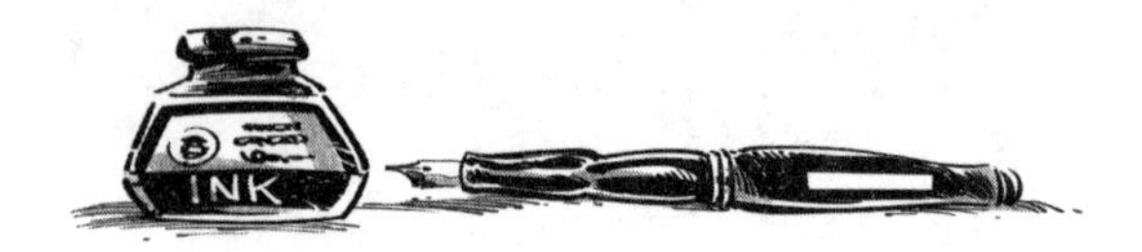

Beth kept thinking about Leza's grandparents. She wanted to help them. But she and Leza hadn't thought of any way to help as they walked to Leza's home. And nothing came to them as they did Leza's chores and ate dinner.

That night she slept in Leza's bed with Leza. Even Beth's dreams were filled with thoughts of Leza's grandparents.

The next morning, Beth pulled the warm

quilt over her shoulders. Finally, she'd had a nice dream. Leza and her family had traveled to the United States. They were safe from the Nazis.

The bedroom door squeaked open. Then there was the sound of a curtain opening. Early morning light poured into the room.

Leza's mother said in a cheery voice, "It's time to get up."

Beth sat up. She blinked.

Leza moaned.

"Breakfast is on the table," Leza's mom said.

Leza and Beth got out of bed and dressed quickly.

"Race you down the stairs," Leza said. Beth laughed and took off running. Leza's long legs won the race.

"What a ruckus," Grandma Pearl said. She stood at the bottom of the steps. Grandma Pearl was kissing Leza on the forehead when

Beth arrived. "I've made buckwheat pancakes and my special blend of tea."

The kitchen was small. But there was enough room for Beth, Leza, her mom, and grandparents. Her father was already gone.

"You're here, and there are buckwheat pancakes!" Leza said. "Are we celebrating something?"

"We are celebrating your new passport," her mother said.

"And today, we may get a passport too," Grandpa Ben said. "Then Sempo may give us all visas."

Beth took a bite. The pancakes were warm and delicious.

"Thank you for breakfast," Beth said when she was done.

"What good manners," Grandma Pearl said.

"Thank you for breakfast," Leza said.

Leza's mother laughed. "You're welcome. Leza, you and Beth go to the Japanese consulate," her mother said. "Save us a place in line."

"Where's Father?" Leza asked.

"He's closing his shop and packing his tools," Leza's mother said.

"It's a shame no one has bought his shop," Grandpa Ben said.

"Perhaps someone still will," Leza's mother said. "But he must take what he'll need for his new job in America."

Leza and Beth took their plates to the sink. Then they left through the front door. They walked in the shade of birch trees that lined the street.

"I thought about your grandparents all night," Beth said.

"So did I," Leza said.

"What if they don't get a passport?" Beth asked.

"They will," Leza said. "Then we'll all leave together."

Beth hoped that was true. "But . . . ," she said.

"All we can do is hope and try," Leza said. "We can't stop hoping. We can't stop trying. And we won't take no for an answer."

Dear God, Beth prayed, *please help Leza's grandparents get a passport and her family get visas.*

The girls passed many homes. They passed the bakery, the fresh-fruit stand, and the butcher shop.

The door of the butcher shop opened. "And don't come back," a man in a dirty white apron said. He threw a girl around Leza's age out the door.

Beth recognized her. It was Gabby, the girl from Grandma Pearl's tea shop. Gabby landed on the cobblestones with a thump. Her hands

hit the ground. Her brown dress rose above her scraped knees.

Then the butcher tossed a handful of coins at her. “I don’t want your money,” he said. The sound of laughter came from the shop. The butcher slammed the door shut behind him.

Beth and Leza helped Gabby to her feet.

“What happened?” Beth asked.

“I guess Jews can’t buy lamb shanks,” she said. There were tears in her eyes.

Leza scooped up the coins from the ground. “Jews *can* buy lamb shanks,” Leza said. “Just not here.”

“It’s wrong that the butcher won’t sell meat to you,” Beth said. “I’ll get the lamb shank for you.”

Leza grabbed Beth’s arm. She said, “Don’t go in there!”

Beth knew she might be thrown out of the shop too. But she had to try.

Beth's Testimony

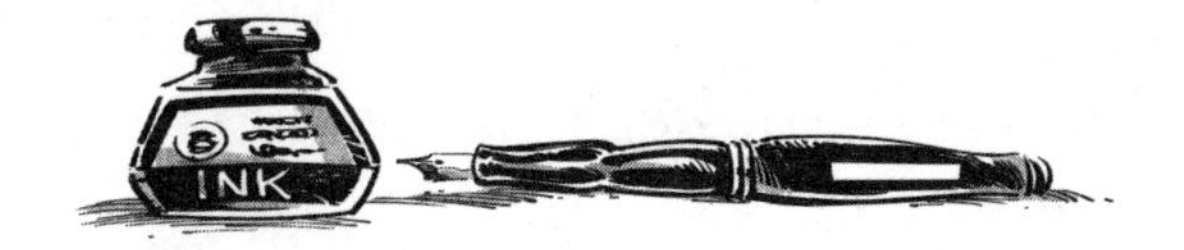

Gabby stood in Beth's way. Gabby said, "I will go somewhere else."

"I'm Jewish too. I'll take you to a Jewish butcher's shop," Leza said.

"No!" Beth said. She took the coins from Leza and marched into the shop. She pushed to the front of the line. Then Beth put her coins on the counter. "A lamb shank, please," she said.

The shop suddenly grew quiet.

The butcher's eyes grew dark and angry. "I don't serve your kind here," he yelled.

"You don't serve Christians?" Beth asked. "I know you don't serve Jews. Who do you serve?"

"You're not a God-fearing Christian," he yelled.

"I am," she said.

"How dare you," the butcher said. He slammed a sharp knife down on the counter. Its point stuck in the wood.

Beth took a deep breath. "I believe Jesus Christ is the Son of God," she said. "He died on the cross for my sins and yours. He rose after three days."

Someone in the shop gasped. "I believe that too," he said.

Beth stared into the butcher's eyes. "I made a choice to follow the one true God. I believe in God the Father, God the Son, and God the Holy Spirit. One God made up of three Persons," she said. "There is no other god."

Someone behind her grunted his agreement.

"She *is* a Christian," a customer said before Beth was finished. "Do you serve Christians?" he asked the butcher.

The butcher's eyes narrowed. "Of course I do," he said. "But she's going to give the meat to that Jew out there."

"I'm giving my mean mother-in-law a steak from your shop," a man said. Others laughed. "Does that mean you won't sell to me?"

Beth waited.

The butcher frowned. He wrapped up a lamb shank. He took the coins on the counter.

"Thank you," Beth said and then left the shop.

Beth gave Gabby a smile and held up the lamb shank.

"How did you do that?" Leza asked.

"Why would you do that?" Gabby asked.

Beth handed her the paper-wrapped meat. "I helped because I could," she said.

Gabby took the meat.

"We're going to the Japanese consulate," Leza said. "Maybe your family should go there too. They might be giving visas to Jews."

"I'll tell my family," Gabby said. "Thank you." She smiled and left.

The girls started walking toward the consulate again.

"Beth, you were very brave," Leza said.

"I did what I knew was right. But the butcher could have thrown me out too," Beth said.

"I'm glad he didn't," Leza said.

The girls reached the consulate. But there was already a long line. They hurried to the back.

"Look!" Leza said excitedly. "The line is moving."

"They must be giving out visas," Beth said. "This is wonderful!"

The girls laughed.

"Let's play a game while we're waiting," Beth said.

"I Spy," Leza said. "I spy with my little eye something black. Now you guess what I'm seeing."

"That car," Beth said.

"No," Leza said.

Beth looked around. She asked, "That man's small hat on the top of his head?"

"Yes, that's right. The small hat is called a kippah," Leza said. "He wears it to show respect for God. Your turn."

Beth said, "I spy with my little eye something white."

Leza looked around. She said, "Is it that tallit?"

"I don't know what a tallit is," Beth said.

Leza laughed. "Is it that white shawl with knotted fringe that man is wearing?"

"Yes," Beth said.

"Men often wear the tallit as they say their morning prayers," Leza said. "Look, there are my parents."

"Over here," Beth called. She waved her arms.

Leza's parents walked over to them.

"How did it go?" Leza asked.

Leza's father looked sad. "My clock shop is closed," he said. "Your grandparents are at their tea shop. They're closing it also."

"Do they need help?" Beth asked.

Leza's mother said, "You two may go help. But come back soon. You'll need to get a visa stamp on your passport."

"Okay," Leza said.

The girls hurried down the street, away from the line.

Patrick looked at the line. No matter how many visas Sempo wrote, the line only grew longer.

But Sempo didn't complain, so neither would Patrick. He took the fee, wrote down names, and passed out numbers.

Everyone was patient. But they looked weary.

A couple came forward. Patrick recognized Leza's father and mother. Patrick looked behind them for Beth and Leza. But they weren't there.

Boris stamped the passport of the couple.

But Sempo didn't write on it. "You are not from Poland," he said.

"No," Leza's father said. "We're Lithuanian citizens."

Sempo looked down. "I'm sorry," he said. "I can't help you."

"Why not?" Patrick asked.

"I can't issue a visa to a Lithuanian citizen," he said. "I don't have the authority. I can only give visas to refugees from other countries."

Leza's dad nodded. He picked up his passport. Then he and Leza's mother walked away.

Patrick ran after them. "Wait," he said.

Leza's father turned around.

"Will another consulate give you a visa?" Patrick asked.

"No," Leza's father said. "The other consulates have closed. Sempo is our last hope."

"And Sempo said no," Patrick said.

"Today he said no," Leza's mother said. "The next time we come through, he may say yes. So, we go back in line."

Patrick watched Leza's parents leave.

Would Sempo say yes the next time they came forward? he wondered. Patrick hoped so. But he doubted it.

The Tea Shop

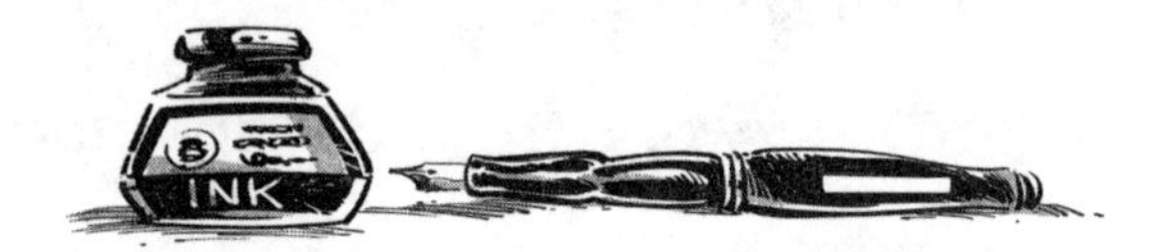

Beth and Leza opened the front door of the tea shop.

"Grandma Pearl?" Leza yelled. "Grandpa Ben?"

"We're in back," Grandpa Ben's voice yelled.

"Come on through," Grandma Pearl called.

The girls went to the room behind the counter. It smelled like cinnamon today.

Grandma Pearl had a white apron on over

her flowery dress. She and Grandpa Ben sat at a small table drinking tea.

"We're almost packed and ready to leave," Grandpa Ben said. He took a slow sip of tea.

There were two suitcases by the back door. A cloth bag overflowing with tea packets was next to them.

"We came to help," Leza said. "But we're too late."

Thump!

"What was that?" Beth asked. It sounded like something had hit the front windows.

Grandpa Ben stood. He hurried to the front room of the tea shop.

Grandma Pearl removed her apron. Then she, Beth, and Leza followed.

Thump!

This time Beth saw a rock hit the tea shop's window. The window cracked.

Pearl's Tea

"Stand back," Grandma Pearl said. "The glass might shatter."

Beth heard loud voices coming from outside the store.

"Go home, Jews!" a man yelled.

"Isn't that John?" Grandma Pearl said. "He owns the shop next door."

"Jews are thieves!" another man said.

Crash!

A brick shattered a small window.

Grandpa Ben ran forward. He locked the door. "We're not safe here," Grandpa Ben said. "We need to leave now."

They quickly went through the door to the back room.

Crash!

More glass shattered.

"Get out of our city!" someone yelled.

Grandpa Ben picked up the larger suitcase.

Leza picked up the smaller bag first. Then she picked up the cloth bag.

"Just one more thing," Grandma Pearl said. "My special blend." She turned to go back into the tea shop.

"No," Grandpa Ben said.

Bang!

"That was the front door!" Leza said. Her face turned white.

People were inside the tea shop. Their yelling grew louder.

Beth's hands were shaking.

"Let's go," Grandpa Ben said. "Everyone! Out through the back door! Now!"

The four of them fled into the alley.

"This way," Grandpa Ben said.

Leza took off running.

"Why are they doing this?" Beth asked.

"Our city has turned against us," Grandma Pearl said.

They followed Leza down the alley behind other storefronts.

Beth looked over her shoulder. People were coming out of the back door of the tea shop.

Beth and her friends turned the corner. People were on the sidewalk. Leza and Grandpa Ben ran ahead of them.

"Slow down, Beth," Grandma Pearl said. "You and I can't outrun them. We need to blend in."

Beth didn't want to slow down. But she did. Her heart started pounding. She heard footsteps nearing them.

"There they are!" a voice yelled. Beth passed the butcher shop.

The butcher came out on his step. "What's going on?"

"We're getting rid of Jews!" someone said. "That girl is one of them."

The butcher looked at Beth. His eyes squinted. His mouth closed in a firm line.

Beth's face turned red.

"She's not a Jew," he said. "I've already heard her tell about her Christian faith once today. I don't want to hear it again. Don't waste your time on her."

The butcher went back into his shop.

Keep walking slowly, Beth thought.

The mob faded away.

Beth was so thankful. She was thankful she had helped Gabby. She was glad she had told the butcher she was a Christian. If she hadn't, she and Grandma Pearl might have been caught.

They walked past the fresh-fruit stand and the bakery. Soon they were in a neighborhood with tall trees.

Grandma Pearl said, "Grandpa Ben and I

need to rest at Leza's home awhile. Then we'll all go to the Japanese consulate."

Beth said, "But you don't have a passport."

Grandma Pearl nodded. "The Japanese consul is our last hope. So we will go to the consulate every day and ask. We have to keep trying."

Beth wanted to continue hoping like Leza's family. But she didn't think Sempo would be able to give them passports.

Closed!

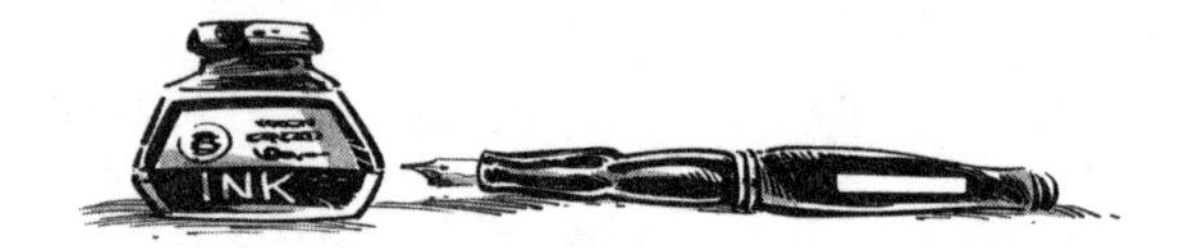

For five days the Japanese consul issued visas. Patrick rubbed his eyes. He, Sempo, and Boris hadn't slept more than four hours each night.

The Japanese consulate was the only consulate open besides the Russian one. The Japanese consulate had given out thousands of visas. But more and more people kept coming.

Boris stamped passports. Sempo wrote and signed. Patrick took the fees. He no longer wrote names in Sempo's notebook. Sempo told him it no longer mattered.

"The Lithuanians are in line again," Boris said. "They've come every day."

Patrick saw Beth, Leza, and Leza's parents. The grandparents weren't with them this time.

"I don't blame them," Sempo said. "I will give visas to anyone who asks now.

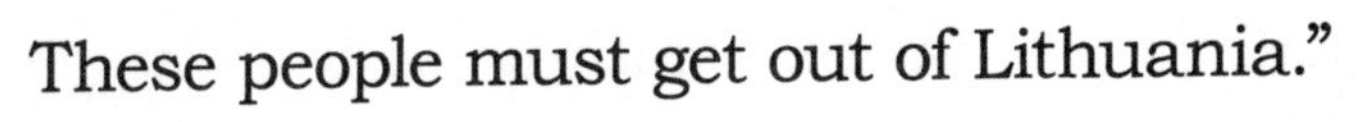

These people must get out of Lithuania."

Patrick waved at Beth.

Beth waved back.

Leza's family would get their visas. He quickly took the fee from the people in front of him.

There were only two families between his

friends and Sempo. He couldn't wait to see their faces when they heard the news.

A whistle blew.

"Go see what's happening," Sempo said.

Boris stood up. He ran past the crowd in the garage and into the backyard.

Patrick took Boris's stamp and used it. Sempo filled in the information and signed it.

Boris came running back. "Russian soldiers are telling people to leave," he said. "They're closing our consulate."

Sempo motioned the next family forward.

Hurry! Hurry! Patrick thought. Leza's family was after this family.

Boris stamped.

Sempo wrote and signed.

Patrick waived the fee.

The whistle drew nearer. Russian soldiers were forcing people to leave.

The line grew shorter for the first time in days.

Sempo motioned Leza's family forward.

Leza's father stepped up to the table. He handed over his passport.

Stamp. Write. Sign.

Leza's father looked grateful.

The Russian soldiers burst through the doors of the garage. Four whistles blew at once. Patrick covered his ears with his hands.

"This consulate is closed," a soldier in a dark-green helmet said.

Sempo handed the passport back to Leza's father.

A soldier pushed Leza and Beth back. He motioned for Leza's father to leave.

Beth leaned forward. "Stamp this," she yelled.

Patrick stretched to get the paper. It was the passport from the Imagination Station. But he couldn't reach it.

The soldiers drew their weapons.

Everyone started to run.

Babies were crying.

An older woman stumbled.

The crowd swallowed Beth and Leza.

Patrick ran after Beth. He lost sight of her. Patrick looked back at Sempo.

Sempo's head rested on the makeshift desk. He was exhausted. He'd done all he could.

"You will vacate these premises," a soldier told Sempo. "The consulate is closed."

Sempo sat up. "As you say," he said.

"Immediately," the soldier said.

Sempo stood. "Boris, please pack these items," he said. "Everything else has been packed."

Patrick ran to Sempo. He put his arm around Sempo's back. Sempo put an arm around Patrick's shoulders.

"Thank you," Sempo said.

They walked to the back door of his house.

Sempo said, "I couldn't help them all."

"The soldiers wouldn't let you," Patrick said.

Yukiko was at the door.

"The consulate is closed," Patrick said.

"I saw," Yukiko said. "Sempo, you are too tired to travel." She put her arm around him.

Patrick let go.

"We'll stay at the Hotel Metropoles tonight," Sempo said.

"Then we'll board a train for Germany tomorrow."

"Germany?" Patrick asked. "Don't you mean Japan?"

"No," Yukiko said. She looked worried. "Japan wants us to go to Germany."

Patrick didn't like the sound of that. Germany wouldn't like what Sempo had done. He would be in trouble there.

"What can I do?" Patrick asked.

Sempo said, "My official stamp is packed. But send a message to the Jewish people. I can give them permission papers at the hotel before we leave. The Russians will honor them like visas."

Patrick nodded. He hurried around the house.

"I should have come sooner with my family," a girl said. "My name is Gabby. Can Sempo help us?"

Patrick nodded. "Go to the Hotel Metropoles tonight," Patrick said. "Sempo will give out permission papers. They are like visas."

"Thank you!" Gabby said.

Russian soldiers came toward them.

"I have to go. I need to tell my cousin Beth and her friend Leza. And others, too," Patrick said. "I only have a few hours before I need to help Sempo."

"I know Leza and Beth," Gabby said. "I'll try to find them too."

"Thank you," Patrick said. He took off at a run. If only he knew where Leza's family lived.

Beth sat at the large table in Leza's home. She went over their situation in her mind. Leza's parents had their passport and visa. Beth, Patrick, and Leza had a passport, but no visa. Leza's grandparents didn't have either.

Leza's family seemed to move in slow motion all afternoon. Grandpa Ben went out to meet his friend Martin. He returned after a short time. No one else left the house.

"We'll make plans tomorrow," Leza's mother said.

Not even the evening meal cheered up anyone.

Beth kept feeling like she was missing something. The names *Pearl* and *Ben* kept coming to mind. She felt so bad that she couldn't help them.

Finally, Grandpa Ben said, "Grandma Pearl and I will remain in your home. Leza and Beth will stay with us. We'll find a way to leave. Then we'll meet you."

"No," Leza's father said quietly. "We leave together, or we don't leave at all."

"You are stubborn," Grandma Pearl said. "But you must get away to make a home for us. You have a job waiting. We need you to take it."

Leza gave her mother a tight hug, and then she stepped back. "You and father can go. So you must go," she said. "The rest of us will sneak out of Lithuania."

Beth's heart started to beat quickly. They were going to have to escape.

Too Late

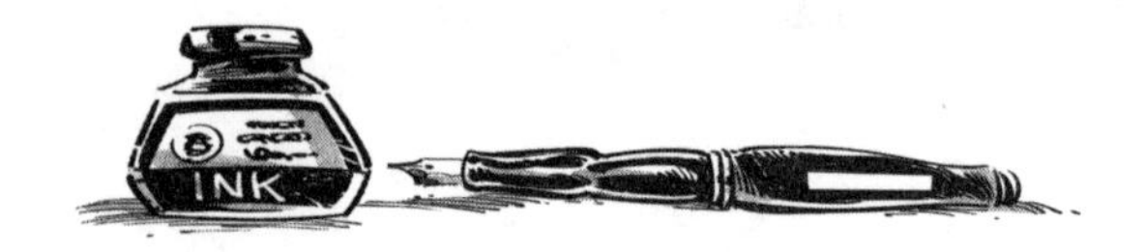

Leza's father started shaking his head. "But we don't want to leave without you," he said. "And we can't leave because we have no money for travel. No one bought my shop."

"Would you both leave if you had the money?" Grandma Pearl asked.

"Yes," Leza's father said.

"So, if you had the money," Grandpa Ben said, "you would leave. I have your word on that."

“Yes. Yes,” Leza’s father said.

Grandma Pearl looked at Leza’s mother.

“Of course,” Leza’s mother said.

Grandpa Ben laid a stack of bills on the table.

He said, “Martin helped me sell our tea shop. We didn’t get what it was worth. But we got enough to travel. This portion is for the two of you.”

Grandma Pearl said, “The money will take you through Russia. It will pay for your traveling expenses.”

Beth felt like crying. Some had to leave. Some had to stay. And both choices were equally heartbreaking.

The evening turned into a long night of talking. Leza’s parents begged her grandparents to release them from their promise. The grandparents wouldn’t.

The next morning, they had a quiet breakfast.

Beth and Leza helped Grandma Pearl wash the breakfast dishes.

Grandpa Ben watched Leza's parents pack.

Leza's mother stopped. "Leza, please go buy a lamb shank at the butcher," she said. "We'll have one last meal together."

Leza nodded.

"You should leave today," Grandpa Ben said.

"No," Leza's mother said. "We'll go tomorrow." Her voice was firm.

Leza and Beth left the house. A morning breeze rushed past them. But the fresh air didn't cheer Beth's spirits.

A girl's voice yelled, "There you are!"

Beth turned.

Gabby ran toward them.

"Hi, Gabby," Beth said. "Were you looking for us?"

Gabby sounded out of breath. "Yes!" she said.

“What’s wrong?” Leza asked.

“Patrick wants you to meet him at the Hotel Metropoles,” Gabby said. “The Japanese consul is giving out permission papers to leave Lithuania!”

“Permission papers?” Beth asked. She knew about passports and visas. She didn’t know about permission papers.

“Yes,” Gabby said. “They work like visas.”

Leza squeezed Beth’s hand.

“My family got ours last night,” Gabby said. “But you have to hurry! The consul is leaving the city by train today.”

Patrick walked across the wooden planks of the train station. He, Boris, and Sempo were only steps away from Sempo’s train.

Sempo didn’t look up.

Boris guided him and held the ink.

Sempo wrote his name on a sheet of paper. Then he held it out in front of him.

A man said, "Thank you."

The man took the paper.

Patrick gave Sempo another sheet. Sempo signed it and a woman took it.

Jewish families surrounded them.

Hiroki leaned out of a train window. "We're here, Father," he yelled. "I've saved you a seat next to me."

"He's coming, Hiroki," Boris yelled back.

The bright morning sun beat down on them.

People in the crowd pushed against one another. But they let Sempo, Patrick, and Boris through.

Patrick handed Sempo another blank sheet of paper. They ran out of permission papers at the Hotel Metropoles that morning. But with Sempo's signature, people could fill in their own information.

The train whistle sounded. They reached the steps of the train.

A man pushed Patrick aside to reach Sempo.

Boris touched Sempo's shoulder. "Goodbye, my friend."

"Goodbye," Sempo said. He turned to the crowd, and he bowed.

"Help us, Sempo," a voice cried. "Don't leave us."

Sempo stepped onto the train. "Patrick and Boris, thank you," he said. "I wish you both the very best."

Sempo bowed to them.

Patrick wanted to thank Sempo for all he'd done. He bowed in return. Boris bowed too.

Boris handed Sempo the ink and pen. Patrick handed him the paper.

The crowd grew quiet. Sempo boarded the train.

"One more," a man with a kippah on his head said. "Sign one more. Please, my family needs to leave."

Patrick felt sick for those in the crowd. They would be stuck in Lithuania. He reached into his pocket.

Sempo had given Patrick a permission paper that morning. It would help Leza, Beth, and him leave.

Patrick drew it out of his pocket.

The man with the kippah snatched the sheet from Patrick.

"Thank you," he said.

"No," Patrick yelled. "I wasn't giving it to you. That was mine."

But the man disappeared into the crowd.

Patrick pushed through people. Where had that man gone? Patrick, Beth, and Leza would be stuck in Lithuania without that paper.

Hiroki yelled out the window, "Thank you for getting him here, Boris! Take care of Mei for me."

"I will," Boris yelled back.

Hiroki's face left the window.

Patrick looked back at the train. Sempo couldn't give him another paper. It was too late.

Hiroki turned back to the window. He leaned forward. He threw a couple of papers out of the window.

A woman picked one up. She yelled, "Sempo has signed it. Sempo is still signing papers!"

The crowd gave a loud cheer.

Patrick cheered also.

The noise of the train's engine drowned out their voices.

Hiroki disappeared. Then he reappeared. He tossed out another handful of paper.

People grabbed at them.

Slowly the train started to move.

More and more sheets were tossed out.

The crowd moved with the train.

Someone in the crowd yelled, "Thank you, Mr. Sempo!"

Patrick moved with the crowd. He had to get a paper.

A Signature

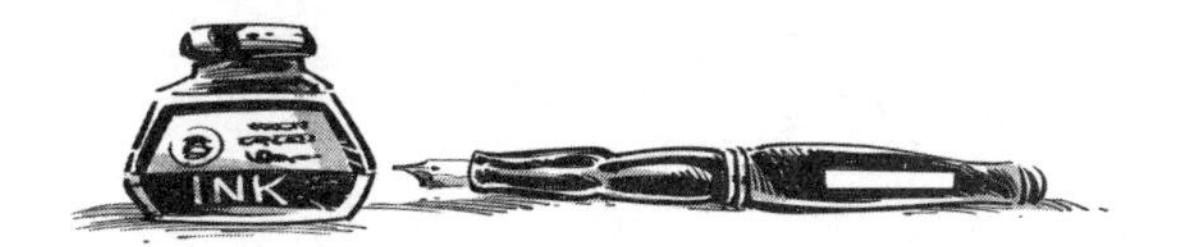

Beth and Leza hurried through the train station. Beth couldn't believe they had missed Sempo at the hotel.

I hope his train hasn't left, she thought.

Beth felt out of breath.

"The train's still here!" Leza yelled. "But it's leaving!"

Papers were flying out one window of the train. A crowd was next to it. They were catching the papers.

The train's wheels began making a slow chugging sound.

Beth saw Patrick in the crowd. "Look," she said.

Patrick tried to grab one of the papers. Someone else grabbed it before he did.

"Let's help Patrick," Beth said. She didn't know what the papers were. But Patrick wanted one, so they must be important. Beth started to run.

Leza zoomed ahead of Beth.

The train picked up speed.

Beth reached the edge of the crowd. She saw Leza push into the crowd.

The train moved faster.

Leza reached the crowd beneath Sempo's window. But Patrick couldn't keep up.

Beth hurried to him. "Are those permission papers?" she asked.

The young boy in the train threw another bunch of papers into the crowd below.

"People can use them like permission papers," Patrick said. "I couldn't keep up with the train. It was going too fast."

They both looked toward Leza.

Leza grabbed for a sheet and missed it. She jumped up to take another. But her fingers didn't grasp it quick enough.

"Only a few people can keep up with the train now," Beth said. "But Leza is one of them!"

The boy threw more sheets of paper out the window.

Leza jumped in the air and grabbed at them. The other people grabbed at the papers too. Leza disappeared in the crowd.

Is she okay? Beth wondered.

The train chugged away at a speed that left everyone behind.

Finally, Beth saw Leza running back toward them. She was waving a sheet in the air.

"She got it!" Beth said.

Leza reached them out of breath.

"You were amazing," Beth said. She looked at the sheet. "Oh no. There's only a signature on it."

"His signature is what's important," Leza said. "It will help us leave Lithuania." But then a sad look crossed her face. "This will work for us with your passport. But my grandparents still need a passport."

It was a quiet walk back to Leza's home.

Once again, the names *Pearl* and *Ben* came to Beth's mind. *What am I missing?* she wondered.

The children entered the front door of Leza's home.

Leza's mom looked up. "No lamb shank?" she asked. "I see you've found a friend instead."

"We have something better than a lamb shank. We have a paper with Sempo's signature on it," Leza said. "It's like a permission paper." She laid it on the kitchen table.

Grandpa Ben smiled. "This is wonderful!" he said. "You children can leave with Leza's parents. We just need to fill in the information for you."

"Let's celebrate with tea," Grandma Pearl said. "Leza, you'll be leaving tomorrow. It's time I taught you my special tea recipe."

Beth felt sad. It felt like Grandma Pearl was giving Leza a goodbye gift.

"I'm not ready to learn," Leza said. "Teach me once we're all safely away from here."

"Nonsense," Grandma Pearl said. She picked up a canvas bag. It was the bag Leza had carried from the tea shop. She rummaged through it and drew out different kinds of tea leaves.

"We are only missing one kind of leaf. But we'll make do," she said.

Patrick drew a paper of tea leaves out of his pocket. "Would Japanese tea leaves help?" he asked.

Grandma Pearl took Patrick's leaves. "That's exactly what I need. This will be our best batch ever," she said with a smile. "Leza, let me show you how this is done."

Leza stood at the cupboard by her grandmother. They sorted and mixed the tea leaves carefully.

Soon Grandma Pearl had Leza pour steaming cups of tea for everyone.

"Thank you," Beth said. She took a sip. It had the delicious taste of peppermint, cinnamon, and apples.

Patrick took his tea to the window. He turned his back to the room. Beth saw him take Whit's gadget out of his pocket.

Beth walked over to him with her teacup in her hands.

Patrick dipped the wand into his teacup.

The green light came on.

"I knew it," he whispered. "The Japanese tea was part of the recipe. The Imagination Station needed the whole mix."

Beth heard the hum of the Imagination Station. She looked out the window. The Model T appeared outside the house.

Then it hit her. *Pearl* and *Ben*. *P* and *B*. *P* for Pearl and *B* for Ben. Beth gave her teacup to Patrick. Then she walked back to the family.

"I have exciting news!" Beth said.

Everyone looked at her.

Beth put her passport on the table. She said, "We have a passport and Leza has a permission paper. They'll work for Grandma Pearl, Grandpa Ben, and Leza. You can all leave Lithuania together."

Patrick was next to her holding their tea. "What is your last name?" Patrick asked.

Grandpa Ben said, "Schmidt."

Beth laughed. "This passport isn't for us," she said. "It's for P. and B. Schmidt and Leza Schmidt," Beth said.

The room exploded with everyone speaking at once.

"What do you mean?" Leza's mother asked.

At the same time Leza's father said, "How can this be?"

Grandma Pearl clapped her hands, and Grandpa Ben laughed.

"But what about you?" Grandma Pearl asked.

"We aren't Jewish. Patrick and I will be fine. But we'll be leaving too," Beth said, "in a different way."

Leza hugged Beth. Then she hugged Patrick.

"What can we do for you?" she asked.

"Take the next train out of here," Beth and Patrick said together.

Sempo's Life

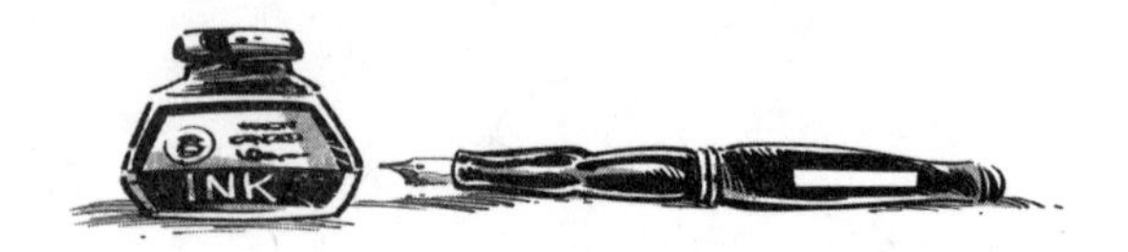

"May we keep this tea and the teacups?" Patrick asked.

"Of course," Leza's mother said with a laugh.

"It's the least we can give you," Grandma Pearl said.

Patrick and Beth waved goodbye.

They left Leza's house, carrying their teacups.

Beth climbed into the passenger seat of the Imagination Station. She turned the key and the compartment on the dash opened. She put in her teacup.

Patrick slid into the driver's seat. He put his teacup in the compartment too. It closed. It was exactly what the Imagination Station needed.

Patrick hit the red button.

Lights flashed. Colors swirled. Then everything went black.

Patrick opened his eyes. He and Beth were back in the basement at Whit's End.

Patrick quickly slid out of the Model T. Beth did too.

Whit hurried over to them. "Are you okay?" he asked. "I was so worried."

"We're fine," Beth said. "We didn't have just one adventure. We had three. First we were in the 1854 cholera epidemic in London."

"Then we were shipwrecked with the apostle Paul," Patrick said. "Finally, we helped Sempo give Jewish people a way to escape the Nazis."

Whit's mouth crinkled into a smile. "Those sound like exciting adventures."

"They were," Patrick said. "But I have a question. Did Leza and her family leave Lithuania in time?"

"Yes, her family escaped," Whit said. "Over 6,000 Jewish people left Lithuania before the Nazis took over."

"I'm so glad," Beth said.

"Their descendants number over 60,000 people today," Whit said.

"What happened to Sempo?" Patrick asked.

"He was sent to prison for two years," Whit said. "Then he returned to Japan in disgrace."

"That isn't right," Beth said.

"No, it isn't. But everyone he helped loved him all of their lives," Whit said. "Then one day a group of them remembered him in a special way."

"How?" Patrick asked.

"Israel gave him the title 'Righteous Among the Nations,'" Whit said. "It's the highest honor a non-Jewish person can receive. Sempo's life wasn't easy. But he served and helped many."

Whit went over and pulled up the hood of the Imagination Station. "Now let me look at the engine's core."

"We found the liquids," Patrick said.

"Tesla's oil came from London. Fruit-seed oil came from Malta. And a special family tea came from Lithuania," Beth said. "Is anything wrong?"

"Not at all," Whit said. "Or as Eugene would say, 'On the contrary.' The glass container is completely filled. I'd better get to work. I need to make a metal container and replace the glass one."

"Beth, let's go upstairs and get ice cream," Patrick said. "I feel like we've traveled around the world."

"Around the world?" Whit said. He laughed. "That's an interesting thought. That could be a whole other adventure."

"I can't wait," Beth said.

Patrick smiled. He hoped Whit changed the core from glass to metal soon.

Secret Word Puzzle

Sempo gave visas to people who needed to leave Lithuania. God gives us something too. Unscramble the letters on the next page. Then write the words on the correct lines on your visa. Next, unscramble the letters in the boxes to find the secret word.

ifel

dlcih

vehaen

ksdae

drol

Date: ______________

____________________ is a citizen of
(child's name)

_ _ _ □ _ _. He/she is granted
(circle one)

passage through this earthly

_ □ _ _ as a _ _ _ _ _ of God.

This is because ____________________
(child's name)

☐☐_ _ _ Jesus to be his/her
(circle one)

_ _ _ _ and Savior.

Signed ____________________________
(child's name)

Secret Word: ☐☐☐☐

Go to TheImaginationStation.com.
Find the cover of this book.
Click on "Secret Word."
Type in the answer,
and you'll receive a prize.

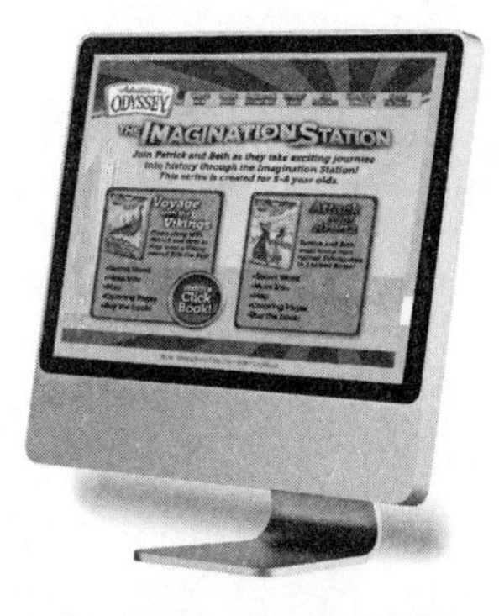

About the Authors

AUTHOR CHRIS BRACK
loves to read all kinds of books, especially kids' books. She, her husband, and her sons share their house with Copper, a basset hound, and Ollie, a huge tomcat.

AUTHOR SHEILA SEIFERT
is an award-winning coauthor of many books, such as *Bible Kidventures: Stories of Danger and Courage*. She likes to find good books for kids to read. Parents can find her bimonthly book flyer at http://simpleliterature.com/bookclub/.